Brave Potatoes

TOBY SPEED

ILLUSTRATED BY
BARRY ROOT

G. P. Putnam's Sons • New York

Library of Congress Cataloging-in-Publication Data
Speed, Toby. Brave potatoes / Toby Speed ; illustrated by Barry Root. p. cm.
Summary: Potatoes set off across the darkened fair grounds to enjoy the rides.
but Hackemup the chef has other plans for them. [1. Potatoes—Fiction.
2. Vegetables—Fiction 3. Fairs—Fiction.] I. Root, Barry, ill. II. Title.
PZ7.S746115Br 1998[E]—dc21 98-16345 CIP AC
ISBN 0-399-23158-7
10 9 8 7 6 5 4 3 2 1 First Impression

To all the fine and fancy vegetables
at the Wayne County Fair, Honesdale, PA,
and to good memories—T. S.

To Samuel Barrett Root—B. R.

Late at night at the County Fair,
when the crowd's gone home and the cows have gone to bed,
all the prize potatoes rub their eyes.

They look to the left. They look to the right.
Everyone's asleep in the Bud and Bean Arena.

So all the prize potatoes with their eyes wide open
        topple to the hard-knocky floor
and one potato, two potato, three potato, four
head for the creak-cracky door.

They sneak past the cabbages snoring in their ribbons,
sneak past the celery and sneak past the leeks.
They sneak out the door and go rolling down the midway—
wide-awake potatoes heading out to ride the Zip.

Way across town at the Chowder Lounge
Hackemup the chef begins attack
with the chopper and the dicer
        and the shredder and the grater
and the masher and the mincer
        and the So-Long-See-You-Later!

See him chop, chop, chop!
Chili peppers on the top.
Spanish onions do a tango while the radishes unfurl.
See the parsnips looking pallid in the Bastaboolabaisse,
while the salad softly sings a veggie-ballad.
See the carrots curli-queuing and the garlic parachuting.
With a plop, plop, plop,
        in the chowder pot they drop!

For his soup
for his stew
for his chowder
and his brew
he's got Maldonada mushrooms.
He's got Bastaboola beets.
For a jumbo jambalaya
that'll set your mouth on fire
he's got armadilly chili,
he's got crocodilly tears.
Pot o' rice
pot o' corn
pot o' carrots
pot o' peas.
He's got green and yellow peppers!
Even royal rutabagas!
EVEN RUBY RED TOMATOES!

But he hasn't got potatoes.
No, he hasn't got potatoes.

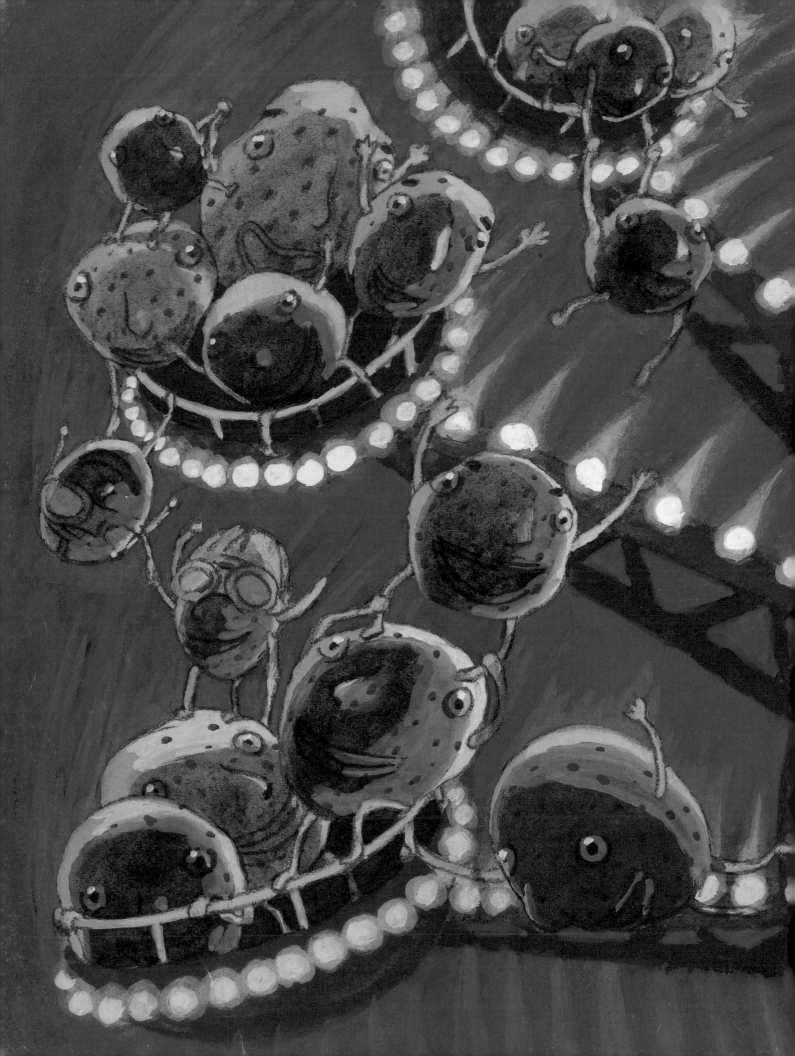

Over at the Fair,
potatoes in the air!
See them flip, flip, flip on the wild and woolly Zip!
See the fearless aviators in their aviating duds
going over, going under in an aerial display.
What a trip, trip, trip! What a perilous ballet
for the mamas and the papas and the wee potato buds.
See the mesmerizing,
            death-defying
                        spuds!

"I think I see, I think I spy
spinning spuds against the sky!
Future hash and curly fries.

"Future chowder, future chips,
future gumbo à la Zip!
Snap them up and let them fry,
snap them up and cook them quick!"

Off goes
        Hackemup
with a bag
        to pack' em up.

"Have you heard the story yet
of Idaho and Juliet?
A spud by any other name
is still a spud, and tastes the same.

"So come to me, my little friends,
tender roots with tender skin,
and I will tell you how it ends
for Romeo and Julienne."

One by one he nabs them.
One by one he burlap bags them.

It's the last stop for potatoes.
Yes, the last stop for potatoes.

"Get in line, potatoes!
Now the end is near!"

The cabbages are quaking. The onions are in tears.
"Better follow orders! Prepare to meet your fate!
It's too late
to be anything
but dinner on a plate!"

But potatoes never listen.
Potatoes have no ears.

See them flip, flip, flip! See them do a double dip!
See the fearless aviators in their aviating duds
as they roll, roll, roll! Brave potatoes forty-fold!

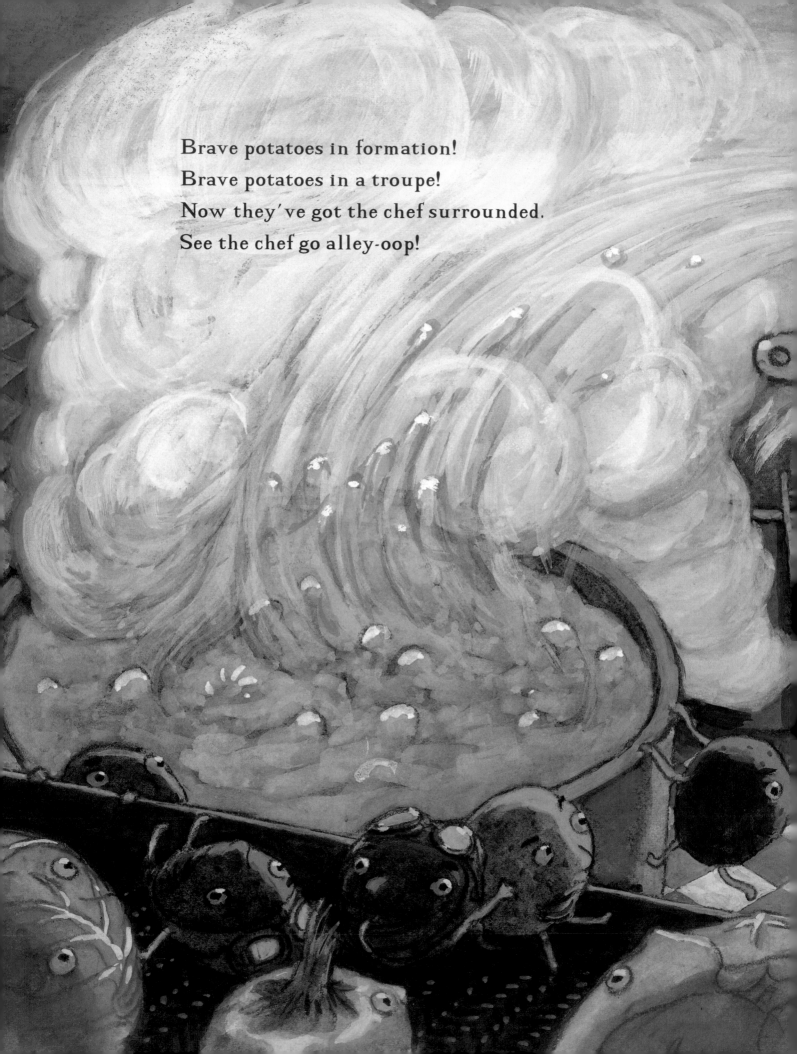

Brave potatoes in formation!
Brave potatoes in a troupe!
Now they've got the chef surrounded.
See the chef go alley-oop!

(It's a puzzle where he's landed. Would you care to taste the soup?)
See the mamas and the papas and the wee potato buds,
see the mesmerizing
        chef-defying
                spuds!

All the other vegetables hop to the floor—
   the ruby red tomatoes
   and the green and yellow peppers,
   the spinach and the scallions
   and the sweet Vidalia onions—
and one potato, two potato, three potato, four
   lead the way to the door.

"We will never be potpie.
We will never be potluck.
We will never be frittata.
We will always be potatoes.

"Potatoes to the finish.
Potatoes to the end.
We will always be courageous.
We will always be potatoes!"